MW00955662

Vampires at Easter

Vampires at Easter

DIARY OF A SNOOPY CAT

R. F. Kristi

Illustrated by Jorge Valle

PRODIGY GOLD BOOKS

PHILADELPHIA * LOS ANGELES

VAMPIRES AT EASTER

A Prodigy Gold Book

Prodigy Gold E-book edition/April 2018

Prodigy Gold Paperback edition/April 2018

Library of Congress Catalog Card Number: 2018

Publisher Website: http://www.prodigygoldbooks.com

Inca Book Series Website: www.incabookseries.com

ISBN 978-0-9984291-1-3

Published simultaneously in the US and Canada

PRINTED IN THE UNITED STATES OF AMERICA

With thanks to

Editor; Amithy Moragoda-Alles

QUIZ TIME:

Connect via:

www.incabookseries.com

If you enjoy this book, please leave a review on Amazon and Goodreads.

Thank you

To Katski

The Inspiration behind the story

TABLE OF CONTENTS

My Family Tree

Queen of Kitties -Inca, the Siberian Detective Cat

Take A Peek @ My Family

INCA (ME):

I am a Siberian kitty, and we Siberians are a pretty good-looking bunch.

I am the natural leader of the Troupe.

There are several reasons for this. After all,

- I am the eldest and the BIG sis of the furry pack!
- I am a super smart kitty!

I bet you, you wouldn't find any kitty smarter than me, even if you swam all the way to China. Mom does not know it, but I AM the TOP STAR around here.

CARA:

Cara, a Siamese kitty, is my pretty sister. She, with the magnificent large blue eyes, is the prissy one in our family.

She is always well-groomed, prim and proper and very attached to Mom.

She is mom's pet. She can do no wrong in Mom's eyes. Yes, Cara loves to suck up to Mom.

Ugh!

FROMAGE:

My brother Fromage is a Tabby-cat. He was named after the French cheese he adores, since fromage means cheese in French.

Fromage loves cheese, any type of cheese, period. He also considers himself a great cheese expert.

Fromage is the mascot of our cheese shop. He goes to the shop with Mom every day. He has built himself a following in the cheese-loving circles of London.

He strongly believes that our cheese shop is a triumph because of him!

Fromage is accident-prone and in the habit of getting into all types of scrapes. If you find something broken in our household, you can bet your bottom dollar that Fromage was behind it!

CHARLOTTE:

Charlotte is a Roborovski dwarf hamster and Fromage's best buddy.

She first met Fromage in our cheese shop in Paris and decided to come with us to London on hearing that we were moving there.

Charlotte is devoted to Fromage despite the number of pickles he gets himself into. I don't understand this friendship between Fromage and Charlotte. Charlotte is intelligent and sharp, whereas, Fromage is??? ... Well, Fromage is Fromage.

Fromage likes to yap non-stop and Charlotte likes to listen. This may be the main reason why they are good friends.

Fromage gets jealous if anyone tries to become too friendly with Charlotte.

MISSY (MOM):

Mom is a humanoid jointly owned by us.

The humanoids call her Missy, but she is Mom to us kitties.

Mom runs our cheese shop. The cheese shop is situated in the heart of Kensington, London. It is modeled on our successful cheese shop in Paris.

We let Mom get away with thinking that she owns us, although it is us kitties who actually own her.

Our world revolves around Mom, but she has a bee in her bonnet about things that we kitties never care about.

❖ Our food

Our diet is carefully controlled by Mom much against our wishes.

No amount of twirling and meowing around her feet can change her mind when she prepares dinner. Even looking at her with adoring eyes gets us nowhere.

Drat!!!! Drat!!!! & Treble Drat!!!

Mom's NO! NO! Food List for us Kitties

No Cream No
Bacon No ice-
cream No Pizza

No good stuff!!!!!!

- Our cleanliness

Mom is a cleanliness freak! When we least expect it, out come our fur-cleaning brushes.

Fromage tries to hide as soon as she gets these brushes out.

But Cara puts on her prissy look and actually purrs when Mom brushes her, her blue eyes blinking like two glorious sapphires - aimed solely at Mom.

Fromage usually snarls "traitor" at her as he dashes under the sofa. But does she care?

NOooo!

I pretend to protest too, but I can't help liking the brush strokes

on my fur. In any case, you can't stop Mom when she gets into her "clean the kitties" mood.

So why not enjoy it?

AUNT FLORENCE:

Aunt Florence is Mom's humanoid Aunt.

I am not shy to say that Aunt Florence dotes on me.

She is the only family Mom has apart from us. Aunt Florence

used to live in the cottage we occupy in Kensington, London. Aunt Florence now lives in Provence, a city in the South of France.

She is an art historian by profession.

Inca and Company, my Detective Agency

I am a super-duper cat detective. Inca & Company is the detective agency that I head. The team has already been involved in solving detective mysteries.

Our fame has spread through London, the rest of England and even reached France.

Inca & Company:

Moi ! Inca - the Head ofthe Detective Agency.

Fromage...My diminutive and energetic Tabby brother, the one who is constantly in a pickle.

Cara - my pretty Siamese sis,the one with the magnificent large blue eyes

Monk - A portly but elegant Blue Russian cat, brainy and sophisticated, companion to Solo.

Charlotte - our beloved and intelligent hamster.

Terrance - A detective doggy by profession. A big powerful dog with a medium length golden coat. He is reputed for his bravery and is owned by Solo,a world famous detective.

Polo - An excitable Pekinese pup, small in stature but absolutely positive that he's a large dog, even though he is not.
He is owned by Raoul and the Señora.

NOW THAT YOU HAVE HAD A PEEK AT MY FAMILY AND MY DETECTIVE TEAM - LET's GET TO THE EXCITING STUFF!!!

Queen of Kitties
Inca, the Siberian Detective Cat

APRIL

14 Days Before Easter

Sunday, Evening

What was all the fuss about?

The word 'Transylvania' had come up several times. Mom was on the phone about Transylvania and there were papers strewn around the dining table about Transylvania.

From glancing at the colorful leaflets, I could make out that Transylvania was a province somewhere in Europe.

The word 'Transylvania' had a nice tone to it
- But we, Mom's family, wondered what was going on.

We had never heard of Transylvania before Mom started getting all excited about this place.

My first instinct was to romp over to Monk's place and have a pow-wow with him and his buddy Terrance. They both lived in a mansion owned by Solo the world-famous detective.

Monk was a dignified Blue Russian cat always sporting a nifty bow-tie.

Terrance was a well-travelled doggy detective. He always accompanied Solo when he was on a case.

If Terrance had not heard about this place, no one else would have.

I was sure of that!

I dashed over to Monk's place with Cara and Fromage trailing after me.

Sunday, Late Evening

We found Monk and Terrance basking in the warmth of the roaring fire in their enormous library.

It was a cold winter's evening.

Solo and his good friend Inspector Reid were hunched over the chess board. They were so engrossed in their game that they hardly noticed us softly slinking into the library.

In any case, they were used to seeing us around as Missy our Mom was a good friend of these two gentlemen.

Fromage had already pushed himself near the fireplace and was stretched out besides Monk whom he hero-worshiped quite unashamedly.

Terrance wagged his tail in greeting, his mouth stretched in a big smile.

I never knew a doggy who smiled like Terrance. "Woof," said Terrance politely when he saw us.

What he actually meant was that it was nice to see us, and his tail wagged furiously. He tends to do this when he sees us.

I am aware that he liked us even though we are kitties.

I got down to business immediately.

"Where on earth is Transylvania? Have you heard of this place before, Terrance?" I asked, my whiskers tingling with inquisitiveness.

I was impatient to get to the bottom of what Mom was all excited about.

She had announced to Aunt Florence on Skype that we would move to Transylvania for Easter.

She had been hired by a wealthy client to cater for an important event in a castle in Transylvania.

Aunt Florence usually spent Easter with us.

I had a habit of eavesdropping on all of Mom's conversations. I had heard Mom inviting Aunt Florence to spend Easter with us in Transylvania, instead of coming to London.

Hearing this, I had broken the news to Cara and Fromage.

I am the nosey one in the family, and I made it my business to know everything that went on in it.

They don't call me 'SNOOPY' Cat for nothing!

Terrance and Monk both looked up in interest and Terrance cocked his head to one side.

“Ah…ha!” he said.

“A very fascinating place though somewhat somber.

“Transylvania is in central Romania. It’s known for medieval towns, mountainous borders and castles.”

“Why do you ask, Inca?” chimed Monk.

“Mom has a gig in Transylvania during Easter,” I responded.

“She has a wealthy client who wishes to celebrate his birthday party with a Monster theme.”

“He has selected Transylvania as his destination.”

“We are planning to spend Easter Sunday and a few days before Easter Sunday, in Bran Castle.”

Terrance sat up, his pink tongue gasped and he looked very attentive all of a sudden.

“Bran Castle!

"Solo once had a case in Transylvania and we had a chance to visit Bran Castle.

"It's a Gothic fortress associated with the legend of Dracula."

"Who is Dracula?" Fromage asked before I could pose the same question.

Monk piped in quickly –"Haven't you heard of Count Dracula?

"The story goes that he was a centuries-old vampire, and a Transylvanian nobleman.

“Unlike the vampires of Eastern European folklore, who are portrayed as repulsive creatures, Count Dracula had been an elegant and charming aristocrat.

“He had also been a scientist and was said to have been very clever with a mighty brain.

“He had studied black magic and it is said that he was no common man.

“He was dead and buried in a great tomb in the chapel of his castle, but according to legend, Dracula had returned from death as a vampire.

“A vampire who sucks blood off humans!”

Monk’s meow had gone deep and hushed while he told us about Count Dracula.

Our collective blood had curdled at his story. Cara gave a whimper and stuttered – “vampires suck the blood off humans!!!”

"What if he sucks the blood off Mom and Aunt Florence?"

"It's only a story, isn't it Monk?" I yowled, alarmed.

Fromage stood up from his comfortable position and puffed out his chest –

"Even if it's not a story, neither you gals nor Mom have to worry about any old vampire.

"I will deal with any vampire who dares to come near you."

Fromage means well, but he is a podgy little soul, full of goodwill but with far too much bravado.

I looked at him sternly –"Thank you Fromage, your help would be welcome."

"Don't forget, I am the eldest and the leader of the Troupe.

"I will take care of Mom, Aunt Florence and all of us and you will be my second- in-command.

"Got it?"

"Right you are sis," he said as he gave me a salute.

"We will deal with any vampire that dares to show his face around us."

Fromage, the brave and heroic army officerhe thought himself to be, saluted his commander after he took his orders.

Fromage had a vivid imagination which more often than not got him and us into trouble.

But he did mean well.

As he accepted that I would be in-charge, I let it pass.

So that was that!

We returned to our cottage. Mom had lit a very nice fire and we wanted to enjoy the heat and take a good snooze.

We were also very interested to hear what Mom had to say about our pending trip to Transylvania.

That evening Monk joined us. Terrance was on duty and had left on a case with Solo.

13 Days Before Easter

Monday, Morning

The news of our departure had spread like wild fire around the neighborhood.

While Mom packed, we had several of our friends dropping in. They wished to say goodbye and wish us 'Bon Voyage'.

I had decided to hold a meeting of Inca & Company - our last meeting before Easter.

Monday, Evening

We met that evening at our usual meeting place – Monk and Terrance's library.

We held our meetings in the Library as it was always warm and silent after Solo went to bed.

Hobbs, Solo's manservant always lit a fire in the great fireplace because he knew that Monk and Terrance spent the night in the Library.

But this evening, the large house was well lit and bright.

Solo had invited Mom over for dinner.

Present at the dinner were Inspector Reid from Scotland Yard - Solo's great buddy; Raoul and his dear wife, the Señora – Polo's Mom and Dad.

It was therefore a full house that evening with the humanoids having dinner in the large dining room while the members of Inca &

Company sat together in the Library.

Terrance had some good news. He had heard that Solo, Raoul and the Señora had alsobeen invited to the party in Transylvania.

Whoopee!

The whole group would arrive in Transylvania a few days before the party with the rest of the guests.

All the guests would be housed at Bran Castle. How thrilling!

I looked forward to meeting my fellow detectives in Transylvania.

Not to solve a crime but to enjoy Easter forgetting all about nasty vampires.

We would have an Easter Egg Hunt!

At Easter, we always ran around our cottage and garden as we searched for the Easter Eggs hidden by Mom.

12 Days Before Easter

Tuesday, Morning

We cats don't generally like to travel.

Actually, the thought of travel gave me the heebie-jeebies.

But I had got used to travelling.

During my short life, we had travelled frequently by car from London to Provence to visit Aunt Florence.

Moreover, as our original home was in Paris, we were used to travelling from Paris to Kensington, London when Aunt Florence lived where we now live.

Cara however detested to travel and had to be calmed down at the thought of it.

Mom had arranged for her two assistants to take over all the specialized cheese and wine that she would need for the party before we arrived.

Jacques and Genevieve, a young French couple, were not only Mom's assistants but also owned shares in Mom's cheese business.

They would prepare the rest of the food for the party, fresh from local produce.

Aunt Florence would come up to London and fly over with us to Bucharest where Mom would hire a van for us to reach Bran Castle.

That was the plan of course, but all good plans tend to have some hiccups.

This was our first plane ride.

Charlotte imagined our first plane ride. She whispered to me –

"Inca, you and I will ride on top of the plane while the rest of the family sits inside.

"I want a chance to have my head really in the clouds."

Little did we know that we would be locked up the whole journey in our small carriers – separated from each other.

Cara who cuddled up to Mom or me when she was nervous, protested loudly all the way from the airport to inside the plane.

Some people in the plane gave Mom dirty looks.

Mom in return glared back and I thought that we would cause a mini uproar in the plane.

Finally, to calm Mom down, Aunt Florence took Cara into the minuscule toilet in the plane and gave her a good talking to.

Cara came back subdued but still alarmed.

She muttered, "Inca you told me that this was just like riding in the car – you were SO wrong!

"My ears are buzz...buzz...buzzing."

Tuesday, Afternoon

Thankfully, the flight from London to Bucharest was not long and we arrived at Bucharest airport in a few hours.

With relief, we settled down in the car hired by Mom and were soon on our way to Bran Castle.

On the way, Mom pointed out the Peles Royal Castle, the former summer residence of the Romanian Royal Family, which was now Romania's most visited museum.

She stopped in Brasov downtown, just to look at a typical Transylvanian old city.

As we peeped out of the window, we noticed that it was a beautiful city, steeped in old world charm.

The journey onwards was peaceful when compared to the plane journey and we enjoyed the pretty countryside in harmonious silence while we listened to French music.

11 Days Before Easter

Wednesday, Evening

It was late evening when we arrived at Bran Castle as we had stopped to have dinner on the way.

Bran Castle was huge - much larger than we had ever imagined.

The castle was perched on a rock.

From the castle you could see the valleybelow with a flowing river.

Aunt Florence who was an art historian by profession seemed to know all about the place.

She said that it was built in the 14th century and had served for ages as a military fortress that controlled the entry route to Transylvania.

It is nowadays frequently associated with Dracula's myth.

I nudged the others with a meow –

"Did you hear that? It's a myth - a make-believe story.

No vapires! No ghosts!

No haunted houses!" Cara was relieved.

But Fromage looked disappointed.

He had hoped to show off his bravery as he protected us from the dreadful vampires!!!

Despite Aunt Florence's belief that Dracula and vampires were a myth, the sight of Bran Castle gave me the creeps.

Our eyes rounded as we drove up to the Castle.

It was ghostlier than we had imagined.

Despite myself, I felt the fur on the back of my neck rise.

Mom on the other hand was thrilled with the place and said "Perfect choice for the party. The guests will be delighted at this spooky castle."

"I am sure the party will be a great success Missy," said Aunt Florence.

"You have chosen the venue well."

All good and well for Mom to be pleased, but I felt in my bones that this was a sinister place.

My sixth sense which was highly developed felt that terror had reigned within the somber walls of Bran Castle.

But I tried to put on a brave face, so as not to alarm Cara and Fromage.

Mom let us out as soon as we stopped.

With Cara practically on my tail and with Fromage close behind, we cautiously jumped out of the car and followed Mom and Aunt Florence to the door of the castle.

Mom lifted and banged the huge scary door knob.

There was an eerie silence. Just as Mom lifted the knob to clang it again, the door quietly creaked open.

A tall lady in a long black dress with a serious pale face stood before us. She held up a candle.

Although she smiled, she had mean and clever eyes and I felt a shiver run down my spine.

I shook myself. I have a vivid imagination and a suspicious mind, sometimes tending to see things where there was nothing.

The lady said in a deep hushed voice. "I am Madam Adela, the housekeeper."

"The lights don't work but the electrician will be here first thing in the morning."

"Your assistants are in the kitchen."

Fromage immediately perked up. He knew that there would be plenty of cheese where Mom's assistants were.

Fromage who loved cheese was anxious to run to the kitchen to supervise Mom's assistants, our friends Jacques and Genevieve.

I grabbed him back –

"Later Fromage. Let's check out where weare going to sleep."

He reluctantly followed me and we trotted after Mom and Aunt Florence.

Madam Adela seemed to float in the air as she led Mom and Aunt Florence to our rooms.

The rooms were enormous. I felt our whole cottage back in Kensington would have fitted into the bedroom Madam Adela had assigned just for Mom and us.

Cara hid behind me and whispered –

"Will a huge and ferocious bear jump out at us, Inca?"

"No way!" I muttered.

I imagined a huge nasty bear in front of my eyes. I couldn't help myself.

"The place is dark and gloomy- that's why Mom has selected this place for the theme of a haunted party.

"But it's a nice comfortable room with plenty of room for us to play."

Charlotte had already started to explore the room.

Charlotte was fearless. Nothing terrified her.

Fromage added, "Look at Charlotte checking the place out for us Cara. You have nothing to worry about."

"I'll stay here until you give me the all clear" she meowed and jumped up on the bed and looked around cautiously.

In the meantime, Mom had started to put our things away as she softly hummed a tune.

Cara seemed reassured by Mom's nonchalance and relaxed attitude.

We all did in fact. We trusted Mom.

If she was satisfied with the place, so were we.

I did my usual walk around the room to do my own inspection.

I sniffed in all the nooks and crannies.

The place smelled of polish and other mysterious musty smells.

After my inspection, I jumped up on the wide windowsill to check out the garden and nearly fell from the perch of the windowsill at what I saw.

The scene outside was strange and I felt the fur on the back of my neck rise again.

The calmness that had settled on me with Mom's humming evaporated in a jiffy.

Was that a grave-yard at the end of the garden?

Who would have a grave-yard right outside a bedroom?

This place seemed weirder than ever.

What a dismal place!

The window was wide open and I heard the hoot of an owl. Then I saw a movement outside and the sound of something moving.

There was rustling as if some much bigger animal was moving about.

I was suddenly panic-stricken.

I took a deep breath and sternly reasoned with myself. There were no dangerous animals around. If there were, Mom would have told us so.

Even so, I felt something was not normal with Bran Castle.

It seemed to me to be more than just a gloomy castle.

Mom fell asleep quickly as she was tired from the long drive.

We all joined her on the large bed and soon fell asleep.

Nevertheless, I felt myself twitch in my sleep, with no idea of the reason for it.

10 Days, Before Easter

Thursday, Morning

Next morning, we followed Mom and Aunt Florence into the humongous kitchen.

The kitchen was the size of a mini-football field.

Mom's assistants had prepared breakfast for everyone.

They sat with Mom and explained what they had done since they came to Bran Castle three days beforehand.

They had visited all the fresh food markets and farms in the neighborhood to place orders for what they needed for the grand party.

The fresh vegetables and fruit would be delivered to the castle two days before the party.

But the dry ingredients would arrive this morning.

I heard Genevieve say that while all was well she had encountered a serious problem.

The French cheese that they had brought over with them had started to disappear.

She had made sure to lock the stock room where she had stored the French cheese. But every morning some cheese had disappeared.

Three days after the cheese started disappearing, Jacques had thrown a major tantrum and nearly come to blows with the local staff in the Castle's kitchen.

Mom sighed with distress.

No way did she want to fall out with the regular staff in the Castle.

It was important to maintain a good relationship with them.

They would need to work in harmony to make the party a success as she counted on them to serve the food while Jacques and Genevieve prepared it.

She had planned to serve delicious French finger foods at the cocktail party.

"I'll speak to Madam Adela", she said with a worried look on her face as she tried to calm down the hot-tempered Jacques.

The mention of the disappearing cheese had made us perk our ears up.

Fromage lived for his French cheese.

The thought of the cheese disappearing anywhere other than to his very own tummy greatly distressed him.

I was glad that we were not around when the cheese had disappeared.

Everyone knew of Fromage's passion for cheese. He would have been accused of stealing the cheese for sure.

I called my fellow detectives to order.

"I will catch the cheese thief, I guarantee that. "I don't want Mom's party to be disaster.

"She was especially hired as an event planner and caterer because of her reputation as the finest cheese and wine caterer in all of London."

Fromage eagerly agreed with me.

No way would anyone get away with the theft of his cheese.

If anyone was to steal Mom's cheese, it had to be him.

Cara nodded her head in agreement. She definitely wished to see the frown leave Mom's face.

It was decided that we would prowl around the kitchen area in the night to see who was stealing our mouth-watering French cheese.

09 Days Before Easter

Friday, 30 Minutes after Midnight

I had promised to wake up Cara and Fromage around midnight so that we could go down together to the pantry to see who was stealing the cheese.

I had stayed up late to record the day's events in my diary while everyone else went to sleep after dinner.

I looked at the large antique clock which hung on the wall and sighed with relief.

Something must have woken me up. I am glad that I did wake up. What if I had slept the whole night through?

But what had woken me up?

I opened one eye and then the other. I pricked up my ears. I laid still and listened in the dark.

The room was dark and I noticed that Mom, Cara, Fromage and Charlotte were sound asleep.

I lifted my head cautiously and slid off the table where I had been writing, as quietly as I could.

I softly crept over to the bed and nudged Fromage awake.

He got up and yawned.

At our whispered meows, both Cara and Charlotte woke-up.

"Let's go everyone" said Charlotte.

Without much ado, we jumped down from the bed and quickly and softly slinked out of the room, careful not to wake up Mom.

We came out of our bedroom. The whole house was in darkness.

We cats are used to moving around in the dark
– but this was a new experience.

The vast hallways and eerie atmosphere gave us the creeps.

I stood and listened.

I was sure that I had heard something. Could it have been a rat?

I had spent most of the previous day with the local kitchen staff who had behaved very well towards us.

Fromage had stuck close to Jacques and Genevieve as they counted the cheese once again.

Cara had gone with Mom to inspect the great hall and Charlotte had gone with her.

The local cooks thought that I was the cat's whiskers.

Well I am not ashamed to admit that I am a good-looking kitty and people generally tend to admire me and my tail which is really fancy.

While I hung around with the locals, I had listened to their chatter. I understood that the villagers believed in evil spirits and ghosts.

Unlike Mom and Aunt Florence and also Monk and Terrance, the locals believed that there were humans who led a normal life during the day.

But at night, when they slept, their souls left their bodies and haunted the village and tormented people in their sleep.

These evil spirits haunted their prey from midnight until the first cockcrow, when their power to harm people faded.

These evil spirits were called vampires, and vampires were supposed to live forever.

They actually believed in Dracula who they thought was one of these evil spirits.

I decided not to tell the others what the locals had talked about.

Surely, I consoled myself, if Dracula was real, Terrance would have known about it.

I decided to trust Mom. She wouldn't have organized the party in Dracula's pad if it were true and not just a local myth.

I repeated to myself – "There are NO vampires – "There are NO vampires – "There are NO vampires."

Despite repeating this mantra to myself, in the gloom of the night in this huge dark castle, I couldn't help feeling a shiver race through me.

I hurriedly led the way as I urged the others to stay close by my side and not venture off by themselves.

We arrived at the kitchen and hid under a table which gave us a good view of the entire kitchen and the pantry.

We were a subdued lot – I guess all the others had the same fears as I did.

But nobody dared to openly speak of their fear– in case the rest of us would laugh at them.

Suddenly we saw a great big orange ball creep into the kitchen.

I heard Cara take a sharp breath – and I quickly placed a paw across her mouth and whispered—"Shhhhhh... Not a meow."

"But that's a cat" whispered Charlotte. Of course, she was right.

I had been blinded by all the talk I had heard amongst the locals.

It was indeed a cat.

A large orange cat or should I say a patchwork cat with shades of white, black, brown and mostly orange fur.

"A Calico" whispered Cara

I thought to myself – a very large Calico at that.

We watched in silence as she expertly opened the closed pantry door using her sharp claws as a key.

She then helped herself to a large morsel of cheese.

Smart gal, I thought to myself.

She ate some of the cheese right away.

She then tied up the rest in a piece of rag and slung it across her neck.

We watched her in astonished silence. She was certainly a cool customer.

We realized that she was about to trot off and rushed out from under the table.

She must have been surprised, but she didn't let out a meow.

She crouched down low and studied us in silence, as if to say, if you want my cheese, you are out of luck buddy – go find your own cheese.

It suddenly struck me that we were actuallyin her castle.

We were in fact in her territory.

I thought it best to take the diplomatic approach and introduce ourselves before we broached the subject of her stealing Mom's cheese.

As usual, the others let me be the spokes-kitty. I approached her and meowed—"Well hello!

"We arrived last night from London.

"My name is Inca and this is my brother Fromage, my sister Cara and our friend Charlotte, a young hamster who lives with us.

Who are YOU?"

My friendly meow and soft purr seemed to prove to her that we were friends and she responded in-kind.

"Hi! I'm Katski. I don't live on this side of the Castle which is let out to wealthy clients.

"That's why I wasn't here to welcome you.

"I live on the far side of the castle, in the tower, which is rather run down.

"No one actually goes there.

"I only came here as I smelled some delicious cheese.

"I don't get a chance to eat such good cheese".

Fromage perked up when Katski mentioned that the cheese was delicious.

"I agree with you that the cheese is delicious" he said.

"This cheese is from France. You couldn't find a tastier cheese anywhere in the world".

Fromage turned to me with a wide grin.

"Who can blame Katski for taking some of our cheese, Inca?" meowed Fromage.

"I have a better idea," I responded.

"Katski! Why don't you come and share our food instead of taking Mom's cheese?

"She needs it for the party that she is organizing.

"You will for sure like what Jacques makes for us. He is a pretty good cook.

"Deal?" I said.

"Hmmm...... Ok", said Katski after she thought it over for a few seconds.

"I do love your French cheese, but since you have invited me to share your own food, let me try it tomorrow to see if it's as good as you say.

"It sure would make a difference from the scraps I eat up in the tower."

08 Days Before Easter

Saturday, Morning

The next day, Katski turned up for breakfast bright and early.

She was not exactly pretty, but she had a smart and colorful coat which caught one's attention.

She was a pretty large cat and Mom noticed her right away.

Mom is a 'cat person' meaning she adores cats. So, there was no issue on Mom's side to set out an extra plate for Katski.

After breakfast, Katski sat down, wiped her whiskers and gave a contented sigh.

"You French do know how to cook," she said.

She then invited us to the garden which was also a graveyard.

In the daylight it didn't look as scary as it had looked from the upstairs window.

We played a good old game of hide and seek amongst the tombstones.

I was curious to see the rest of the castle and asked Katski if she would show us around.

As we had had such a good time together and had shared not only our breakfast but also lunch and dinner, Katski agreed that it was the least she could do for us.

We followed Katski as she led us through our familiar surroundings to a different part of the castle.

I found our own quarters awful and gloomy enough but this part of the castle was gloomier, darker and even more sinister.

It was filled with spiders and bats.

Charlotte dug deep into Fromage's scarf so as not to be visible.

Cara shuddered.

We reached the tower after we had climbed a steep and winding staircase dimly lit by candles.

We reached the top floor and Katski who led the way, turned around and said,

"Welcome, all – this is my home and here is my young humanoid friend – Dracco."

I studied a little boy who seemed to be about 11 years old.

So, this was Dracco!

During the day, Katski had talked about him non-stop.

Dracco was dressed all in black and carried a magnificent red and black cape.

He seemed wise for his age.

He had dark hair and a very pale face.

He had a solemn expression on his face, but his face lit up when Katski came into the room.

He seemed delighted to see that Katski had brought so many kitties to meet him.

When he grinned, there were two long little fangs on either side of his even white small front teeth.

Katski went up to him and placed a piece of cheese at his feet.

So, the rest of the cheese had been for Dracco, I thought.

I had noticed that Katski had saved more than half the cheese she had received for dinner.

"My magnificent bandidata – Katski!" said Dracco with a laugh.

"What have you pinched for me today? "Another morsel of yummy French cheese?"

Katski explained to us that she was Dracco's only friend.

Dracco couldn't stand the light. Hence, he couldn't venture out during the daytime.

He slept in the daytime and functioned at night-time.

I studied Dracco. I realized that he was a sad and lonely boy.

"Where are his parents," I asked Katski.

"His Mom and Dad perished when he was a baby and he was brought up by his uncle.

"It's a long story, let me show the rest of our place and I will explain it all."

We left Dracco to enjoy his cheese in peace and scampered after Katski.

She led us into another large room. This room was even bigger than the one we occupied.

It was steeped in dust and looked as if it had not been occupied for a very long time.

Underneath the dust, we could make out expensive furniture and the walls were covered with rich tapestries and cobwebs galore.

The room contained a library filled with books.

"This is Dracco's uncle's room," said Katski. "We hardly ever come in here," she added. "What a strange bed," remarked Cara.

We looked at the bed in astonishment. Instead of a normal bed, we saw a long box with the inside covered in plush red material.

"Oh, that's not a bed," said Katski with a wave of her paw.

"That's a coffin.

"We sleep in coffins. Much more comfortable," she added, as if it was the most normal thing in the world to sleep in a coffin.

"Let me tell you a story," said Katski.

"You can climb into this coffin it's far more comfortable than the hard floor."

She had already jumped into the coffin, so we also jumped in.

It was very true; the interior of the coffin was really cozy as it was lined with soft and plush material.

"Red is a fashion statement," added Cara.

Hmmm...everyone seemed to be calm. The fear of vampires had diminished for the moment.

"Here is Dracco's story," began Katski.

"He never knew his Mom or Dad as he came to live with his uncle when he was a baby.

"His uncle loved him very much. Dracco was the only other member of his family alive.

"Dracco was the son of his much-loved sister.

"Dracco is the descendent of a generation of Vampires."

We listened aghast!

In Katski's world, there were vampires.

In fact, we were sitting on the bed of a vampire.

Katski noticed our shocked and scared faces and said –

"Calm down and let me finish my story and then you will

understand."

In our dumbfounded state, all we could do was nod our heads in agreement with her.

So, the story continued.

"His uncle had promised his only sister that he would not allow Dracco to become a vampire.

"A vampire gets his full powers at the age of 12.

"In order to keep his word, from the day Dracco was born, his uncle, who was a scientist, had started to prepare a drug to prevent Dracco from becoming a vampire.

"No sooner had he developed the anti-vampire serum, the vampire community got to hear about it.

"Very soon, the head of the vampire community, an evil enchantress by the name of Buja, found out about this serum.

"She realized that her powers over the vampire community would be lost if she allowed

Dracco's uncle to promote this anti-vampire serum.

"More importantly, she had been waiting for Dracco to reach 12 years of age, so that she could initiate him into vampire-hood.

"So, she came over one night when Dracco was only six years old and enticed his uncle with wine to which she had introduced a strong sleeping potion.

"When he fell asleep, she had her minions tie him up and take him prisoner, along with the anti-vampire serum that was lying by his coffin.

"Dracco and I have named these minions – 'Bujions.

"They were pretty harmless minions who enjoyed their wine, their music and playing around, until the day Buja the Sorceress appeared before them.

She had terrified them and made them her slaves.

"It is believed that Dracco's uncle is held prisoner in the dungeon and being subjected to a source of light making him weak and unable to escape.

"As the days get closer to Easter Sunday, Dracco's birthday, he has started to acquire more and more of the qualities of a vampire.

"I have already felt Dracco turning into a vampire. Some sure signs have developed:

- "He can no longer go out in daylight.
- "He can no longer look in a mirror.
- "Most importantly, his teeth have turned into sharp points, especially his canine teeth.

"Dracco will turn 12 on Easter Sunday. On this night he will turn into a full-fledged vampire and there is nothing it seems that I can do to stop it."

Poor Katski!

Our hearts went out to her.

Imagine if we had lost Mom to some evil spirit. The idea was terrifying.

"Tell me Katski, do you know where Buja and her Bujions are holding Dracco's uncle?" I gasped.

"Yes, I do," meowed back Katski.

"But I don't have the courage to go search for him alone.

"Buja has her Bujions guarding him at all times.

"Dracco's uncle is much stronger than all her Bujions put together.

"But they do control the fierce light through a switch.

"No one knows where Buja has installed the light switch.

"No one has had the guts to go searching for it either."

Katski gave a very sad sigh, and I saw tears pouring from the corner of her eyes at the thought of losing her beloved Dracco.

We all looked on in dismay, sad to see Katski so upset.

"Inca, we have to help Katski and Dracco," cried Fromage.

"We can't allow Buja the Sorceress to get her fangs on Dracco."

I looked at the faces before me:

- Plea! - from Fromage.
- Hope! - from Katski.
- Fear! - from Cara.
- Caution! - from Charlotte.

I reflected as to what on earth we could do? This was a whole new ball game.

Never had we dealt with vampires and sorceresses.

The very thought of them had everyone terrified.

Unknown to ourselves, Dracco had entered the room and had heard the whole conversation.

He picked Katski in his arms and petted her saying –

"Hush, my little Bandita, Katski. "Hush, you are breaking my heart."

He put his arms around Katski and buried his face in her fur.

Looking at the two friends together, I knew that we had to try to get Dracco's uncle out of the clutches of Buja the Sorceress and save Dracco.

I looked at the others, and I noticed that we were at one with this thought.

We had all been touched by the love between Katski and Dracco.

We had to do all we could to help them out.

I declared –

"Enough of these tears. We need a plan. "Here's what I purpose.

"Katski, Fromage and I will go find your uncle, Dracco. You will come with us but you will only be a lookout.

"If anything goes wrong – you must get back to our Mom immediately. She will be in the kitchen. Her name is Missy. She will galvanize the troops to come to our rescue, if she believes we are in danger.

"Cara, you will go back and stay with Mom" I said.

"You will be our back up. In case Dracco comes searching for Mom, he will recognize her instantly because you are with her."

Cara agreed instantly. I knew she had been too timid to tell us that she was scared to accompany us. I wanted it to be easier for her to opt out.

Charlotte added quietly –

"I will be useful to you, Inca. I can slip into places none of you can, because of my size."

I realized that she had a very valid point and nodded in agreement.

Fromage quickly added –

"You can stay in my scarf Charlotte. I will keep you safe."

I saw anger creeping into Charlotte's eyes. She hated it when Fromage tried to play protector.

Charlotte had an independent spirit. Before they could argue, I said –"Let's meet tomorrow as soon as the sun disappears."

07 Days Before Easter

Sunday, Night

We left Cara in bed with Mom. She stayed behind, rather glad, and watched us go off together.

We soon joined Dracco and Katski.

There was a gusty wind outside, and I who didn't like the cold at all, wrapped my scarf tightly around my neck.

I was pleased that Charlotte was hidden deep in Fromage's scarf with only her ears peeping out.

This way, we could also make faster progress. No way could she have kept up with us.

All was in darkness.

Dracco had a small torchlight to guide his steps.

He didn't seem to need it. His vampire origins were developing fast.

I felt that the wind had become sharper and more intense.

The whole group felt themselves shiver. We huddled in a cluster as we groped our way in the dark in order to heat ourselves with each other's bodies.

I was glad Dracco and Katski were with us. We would never have found our way by ourselves.

I looked around for shelter. There was none.

I couldn't control my shivers.

I followed just behind Dracco. After me came Fromage with Katski at the rear.

Dracco suddenly stopped and we all crashed into one another.

He switched off his torch, silenced us with his arm and motioning us to keep quiet.

We were in a grave-yard. We huddled together behind a large tombstone.

Long and low howls filled the air.

It was a pack of wolves in the distance howling for the dead.

We stayed in this position without daring to breathe.

No one wanted to meet a wolf pack.

The howls of the wolves gradually faded away as they moved on.

Dracco wouldn't let us move.

We crouched for a good thirty minutes.

In any case, none of us could move – we were that terrified.

I didn't dare look at the others, as fear had gripped my heart.

There was total silence and the moon peeped out from behind a large shadow.

Dracco slowly got to his feet, and with a signal from him, we started to move again.

We stopped a good thirty minutes later and observed a great big tomb of black and white marble.

The moonlight shone above and there seemed to be no one about.

Dracco whispered to Katski-

“The entrance is through that great tomb. “Good luck and take

care.”

We slowly approached the tomb as we followed Katski’s lead.

Dracco watched us go anxiously.

I knew he wished he could come with us. But he realized that his presence would have been more noticeable.

We were all small in stature and had more of a chance to blend in without catching the notice of the Bujions.

Katski had told me that in the night the village cats often hunted for mice in this large grave- yard and that the Bujions were used to seeing cats roaming about.

Katski had asked us to leave our shawls and Fromage his beret behind with Dracco so that we would look like any other village cat hunting for mice.

Charlotte clung on to the fur on Fromage’s neck since he now wore no shawl or hat.

We silently approached the tomb and slipped inside.

I wondered why it was unprotected. There were no Bujions

about.

I felt my heart pound.

We slowly crept forward following Katski.

We stood and listened, hardly daring to breath, expecting to see the Bujions guarding the entrance.

We could hear no sound other than the rustling of the leaves on the trees.

It was a dark and cloudy night.

Escaping the sharp cold wind outside, we slowly started moving inside the tomb. I realized that there was a long corridor inside the tomb.

Katski led the way through a cave into a passage with a low roof.

The passage inclined upwards and led us right into another old and unused castle.

We soon discovered why the entrance had been left unattended.

At the end of the tunnel, there was a wide- open space.

Through the tomb, we had walked right into the great hall of a castle.

We looked out on an enormous hall paved with flat stones. Weeds were sprouting out of the crevices and cracks in these stones.

We saw at least a hundred small Bujions gathered together in the large hall.

They looked very strange to my eyes.

I had never seen such creatures before.

From behind the rock we were able to watch the goings-on in the great hall.

Hardly daring to breath, we watched thisgang in silence.

They looked like monkeys, but they were not monkeys.

Their faces looked like monkeys but their bodies looked like rodents.

It looked as if they were waiting for something to happen.

A loud clap of thunder made us jump.

Even the Bujions were terrorized. Their smiling faces changed collectively to one of great fear.

We soon found out why.

A regal shadowy figure appeared all dressed in black.

It was a woman's figure, a black shadow,
floating in the air.

The Bujions who had been bickering and laughing amongst themselves seemed to have also collectively lost their chirpy voices and happy faces.

They bowed down low and it looked as if they didn't dare raise their heads in front of her.

We had a tremendous shock. We stood rooted to the spot.

The ghostly figure had gone into a frightening fit.

Suddenly, half of her was facing frontwards and other- half was facing backwards.

She slowly rotated, terrorizing her Bujions. She looked gruesome.

My heart was having a difficult night.

I felt it start to freeze over and reminded myself to breath in and out slowly.

Katski eyed us with a paw to her mouth asking us to be silent and with her head motioned us to follow her.

We followed Katski faltering. Where on earth were we going?

Daring not to breathe, we slowly backed out from behind the ledge that had been hidingus and followed Katski out of there.

It was a relief to be out of the presence of that black floating creature.

Katski huskily meowed that she was – "BUJA THE

SOCERESS."

Katski had been wise to use this moment to go searching for Dracco' s uncle.

The Bujions were all busy pandering to Buja the Sorceress's needs.

Where were we to look?

The place was enormous. It would take us ages if we had to go searching from room-to-room.

Someone was sure to see us.

I said "let me think this through –

"What is the most secure place in the castle, Katski?

"You should know as you have been living in a castle all your life.

"If you had to hide someone or something – where would you put him?"

Katski replied without hesitation. "Definitely in the dungeon.

"In the tower, he could see out.

"Anywhere else in the castle there is more of a chance for him to escape. Particularly as vampires have the power to turn into bats and fly away."

"Good thinking," I meowed. "Let's get moving."

No one needed a second invitation. With a burst of energy, we all charged down to the dungeon.

All castles in this region seemed to have the same architectural design.

With not too much difficulty – Katski was able to take us down to the dungeon.

There were only two large rooms in the dungeon.

One room at the end of the dark corridor seemed to be some sort of office or room where the guards stayed.

The other was what we had been looking for.

We found Dracco' s uncle laid out in a casket deep in sleep with his arms crossed on his chest.

Since he had been kidnapped by Buja the Sorceress when Dracco was just 6 years old, it was hard to imagine that he had been asleep such a long time.

She had got her Bujions to drag him into the dungeon of her

castle. A castle that nobody inhabited other than herself with her legion of terrified Bujions.

Katski who remembered Dracco's uncle well, told us that he looked exactly the same.

I studied Dracco's uncle carefully.

He was very pale with jet black hair pasted against his scalp.

There was a harsh spotlight over him.

I guessed that this was the strong light Katski had spoken about – the light used to keep him immobile and helpless.

Charlotte spoke up excitedly –

"If we get that spot light away from him, I have a feeling we can wake him up again.

"There must be a special reason to have such a strong light directly focused on him."

"You are right," I said.

I was glad Charlotte was with us. She is a very intelligent hamster.

I looked at Charlotte thoughtfully. "You have very sharp teeth,

Charlotte.

"Do you think you could chew through those wires?

"It's the wires that are passing the electricity to the spot light.

"If the connection is disabled, I am sure the light will go off!"

Before Fromage could start to protest that it was too dangerous, Charlotte sped up the jagged wall and started chewing at the wire with all her might.

We suddenly heard a noise.

After pandering to Buja's needs, some of the Bujions who guarded the dungeon were coming towards the guard room carrying a huge jug of wine between them.

Katski dragged us under some old gunnysacks just in time.

Charlotte was still up on the wall chewing the wire with all her might.

She was a tiny creature and the guards who boisterously talked amongst themselves didn't notice her busily at work chewing on the wire.

They were more concerned with making sure that the large jug containing the wine did not spill.

I signaled for Charlotte to stop chewing until the guards settled down and started drinking their wine.

Nobody was around other than the guards. We could see them at a distance in their guardroom.

They were busy playing cards, shouting at each other and continuously filling their mugs with wine from the jug.

It looked to me as if there was a competition to see who could finish their mugs first.

Very soon, they were completely sozzled with the sweet-smelling wine.

I gave Charlotte the signal to resume chewing again.

Charlotte had very sharp teeth.

The strong light shining over Dracco's uncle's body was gone in a flash.

There was a deadly silence, and Charlotte scrambled down the wall and quickly climbed onto Fromage's neck.

Fromage sighed with relief to have his tiny friend back with him again.

"Bravo! Charlotte. Jolly well done," I whispered.

We sat still under the gunnysacks, holding our breath, wondering what would happen next.

We couldn't take our eyes off the coffin, terrified as well as mystified at the situation we found ourselves in.

I, for one, wished to have the stories I had heard from the local castle staff proved wrong.

But at the same time, I desperately wanted Dracco's uncle to

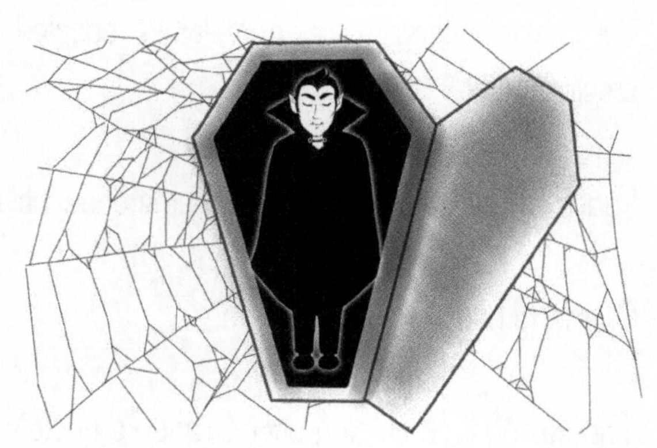

come alive again.

He had to save Dracco from becoming a vampire as he had promised Dracco's Mom.

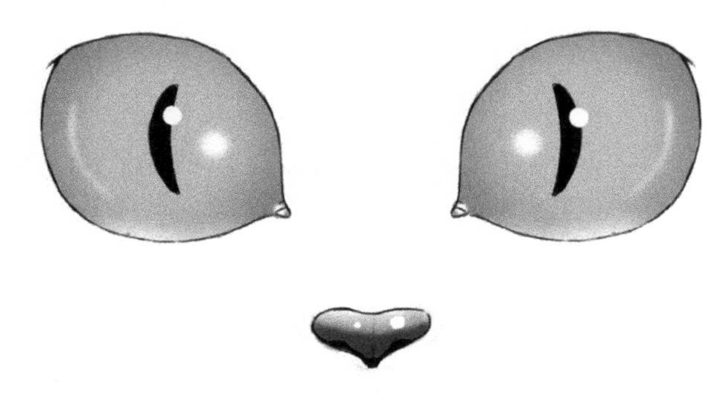

06 Days Before Easter

Monday, About 2 a.m. in the morning

I sensed that morning would break in a few hours.

Soon the sun would come out and Dracco would not be able to stay outside. He would be forced to run back home to Bran Castle.

The guards, after a heavy night of playing cards and fighting amongst themselves while drinking their wine had fallen asleep, one on top of each other.

For the moment they seemed to be dead to the world.

We had slowly crawled out from under the gunnysacks.

Katski went over to the coffin followed by us.

Katski started to lick the face of Dracco' s uncle.

It looked to me as if Katski was willing him to get up.

Katski knew Dracco's uncle very well.

It was he who had collected Katski from a village farmer to keep Dracco company.

Out of sheer desperation, Katski started chewing his ear.

Suddenly a low voice said –

"What are you doing Katski? You know you are not allowed into my coffin.

"I see you have also brought some friends to see me."

It was the uncle speaking.

Katski started jumping up and down on his chest in glee.

The uncle gently lifted Katski off his chest and looked around him.

It was dark with no light around us.

But we could see him well, as we were cats.

You may be aware, us cats can see better in the night than during the daytime.

As we were watching him, we saw that it was as if a light bulb had been switched on in his head, as the past came rushing back to him.

He said –

"My word, Katski – I was never so pleased to see anyone in my life!?

He asked us to get down from the coffin and as we did, before our very eyes, we saw him floating out of the coffin.

We gasped in astonishment while Katski just smiled like a Cheshire cat – grinning from ear- to-ear.

Katski seemed very proud to be associated with Dracco's uncle.

Dracco's uncle gracefully landed on the floor.

He signaled us to not make a sound with a finger to his lips as he went around the room as if looking for something.

Of course, I realized that he was searching for the anti-vampire serum.

He wouldn't want to leave without it.

He hadn't forgotten his promise to his sister to save Dracco.

He said to Katski –

"Buja the Sorceress has the vial of serum "All of you - quickly out of here.

"Go and wait for me outside the tomb and I will follow you soon."

There was a flash of lightening – and before our eyes, Dracco's uncle turned into a large bat.

Could we be more astonished in one night? - I thought to myself.

I rubbed my eyes and pinched myself thinking that what I was seeing was not real.

Nope, I was wide awake.

I shook myself out of my stupor.

Fromage yelped – "Stick a fork in me, am I awake?

"Let's go," said Katski as she urged us to follow her quickly.

I pulled myself together and looked at Fromage and Charlotte.

They too looked bemused, but I noticed the excitement on

Fromage's face.

I knew what we would have to put up with for the next couple of months.

It would be –

FROMAGE THE VAMPIRE TURNED SUPER BAT.

We didn't have much time to think though.

We quickly followed Katski out of the dungeon, up the stairs and through the corridors of the castle to the tomb.

It was about 3.30 a.m. and we found the Bujions guarding the tomb entrance fast asleep.

Buja the Sorceress would give them all a beating when she found out that Dracco's uncle had escaped, I thought to myself.

Suddenly it dawned on me –

What if Buja the Sorceress caught the Bat trying to steal the serum and jailed him once again?

HORROR OF HORRORS!

Shaking this thought from my head, I crept past the guards with the others and went dashing to the rock where we had left Dracco.

No sooner had Dracco hugged Katski and then us in relief, the large bat swooped down on a tombstone and watched us gravely.

Before our eyes the bat slowly turned back into Dracco's uncle.

"UNCLE!" shouted Dracco with joy.

"My Boy!" said his uncle enveloping Dracco in his long arms.

We stood by silently watching the happy pair.

Katski's eyes were gleaming. I suspected atear or two were

about to fall.

"Let's go home," said Dracco's uncle and without another word we followed them back to Bran Castle.

The night seemed to have suddenly become much friendlier.

05 Days Before Easter

Tuesday, Late Evening

"All's well that ends well," I told Cara after I had related last night's episode to her.

We had slept most of the day after which we had a very good dinner.

We were now sitting together on the bed recapping what had happened in detail once again with Cara.

We had not actually solved a mystery but the adventure had been thrilling.

Frightening but thrilling!

Katski hadn't joined us for dinner, but it was understandable.

Today was the first day that Dracco's uncle had returned to Bran Castle and they must be celebrating dinner together, we thought.

Fromage said –

"Let's go visit them tonight!

"Cara will get a chance to meet Dracco's uncle. "Perhaps he will

turn into a bat in front of us." Cara enthusiastically meowed –

"Yes, yes! Please Inca let's take a walk over to Katski's side of the Castle.

"I saved a piece of cheese for her from my share at dinner."

Tuesday, Night

I nudged everyone awake after Mom had gone to sleep. We softly slipped out of bed and cautiously stepped out of our room.

I suddenly stiffened from head to tail. I couldn't move. I was turned to stone.

Something was coming our way.

Rustle, rustle! Scrape, scrape!

Was it a rat?

Would a rat dare to do that?

"Quick, hide," I meowed as we heard soft movements coming our way.

We pushed each other behind a large urn, our hearts batting so loud that I hoped whoever was coming towards us would not hear it.

I sighed with relief.

It was only the housekeeper, Madam Adela softly walking on tiptoe with a small candle in her hand.

She passed by without noticing us. I whispered –

"She is probably making her last rounds before she goes to sleep.

"Let's give her a little time to settle down before we continue."

After some time, we raced each other over to Katski's place.

The musty staircase seemed to be cleaner and the large number of cobwebs seemed to have disappeared.

Cara and I nodded in approval.

Things seemed to be improving already with the return of Dracco's uncle.

Fromage of course had no interest in such things and would not notice if cobwebs grew out of his fur.

As we reached the landing we met Dracco sitting on the top step with a young girl.

She had large blue eyes akin to those of Cara and a mop of black hair.

She was dressed in a nifty short black dress.

She looked really cute.

Dracco seemed to be thrilled with her.

We saw them laughing together and enjoying each other's company.

She turned her mischievous eyes towards us and said with a laugh –

"More of your friends, Dracco. "How delightful!"

Dracco responded –

"These are Katski's friends, and yes they are my friends too.

"They helped my uncle escape from the dungeon of Buja the sorceress."

"Hi, I am Ivy," said the pretty girl.

We looked around for Katski and Dracco said—"Katski went with my uncle to the village to get more food.

"My uncle was outraged to find the pantry empty.

"He likes his food, does my uncle," he added with a chuckle.

"You are all invited for a meal of typical Transylvanian delights tonight.

"Ivy, I am sure my uncle will be enchanted to meet you.

"He noticed that I didn't have any friends and he would be so pleased that I have found a great pal."

Leaving Dracco and Ivy to continue with their fun conversation, I went with the others to check out Dracco's uncle's room.

Everything remained much the same, but the place was very much cleaner and all the cobwebs had disappeared.

The main difference was that we found very many more bats peacefully sleeping upside down, hanging from the ceiling.

Charlotte was pulling at my shawl. "What's it Charlotte?" I meowed.

"Don't like the bats and want to go back to our room?"

"It's not that Inca," responded Charlotte. "I wonder how Ivy found Dracco."

"She's very pretty, isn't she?" said Cara.

"Yes, she is," I said, "but it's true what Charlotte says –

"How did she find Dracco?"

While we were whispering to each other, Dracco and Ivy came into the room.

Dracco was giving Ivy a tour of their quarters.

Ivy casually went about the room admiring the expensive furniture and tapestry that was all cleaned up and beautiful.

After Charlotte's suspicious question, I was watching her carefully.

She was a cheery and bouncy girl with a soft, sweet voice like a tinkling bell.

Dracco was clearly delighted to find a new friend, a charming and pretty friend at that.

She tripped around the room excitedly, admiring the furniture and running her delicate hand on the expensive and valuable tapestry.

Just then Katski came into the room and looked very pleased to see us.

Dracco was distracted with Katski's entrance and as he usually did, picked her up and placed her on his shoulders.

Just then a deep voice said – "I'll take that young lady."

We all turned to look at what was happening.

It was Dracco's uncle who was standing there with his arm stretched out to Ivy.

We saw that Ivy had discovered the anti- vampire serum and had it firmly in her hand.

Dracco's uncle rasped in a loud and commanding voice –

"I KNOW IT'S YOU, BUJA!

"Come out from under your false skin and show us your true colors!"

With an angry 'HZZZZZ' a black whirlwind shaped cloud surrounded Ivy.

Before our astonished eyes Ivy was transformed into Madam Adela.

"Madam Adela," I meowed.

"How is this possible – Ivy and Madam Adela are one and the same person?"

Madam Adela gave a loud cackle and shrieked–

"Catch me if you can" and ran for the door.

Dracco and his uncle stood surprised at her audacity.

Dracco clearly alarmed that his new friend had disappeared and that she was actually Madam Adela had sunk to his knees with his hands across his eyes. His uncle had bent down to calm him.

Katski who had been near the door chased after her first.

Realizing what Katski had in mind, I followed close behind her.

All the animals in the room followed Katski and me.

Madam Adela was fast-footed and she ran rapidly away from us.

But she hadn't reckoned with us kitties.

Although I am not big, I am very quick and agile.

I leapt with one bound onto her back and dug my sharp claws into her back. She staggered and at that moment Katski caught up with her and placed herself in front of her.

Madam Adela not seeing her in time tripped and fell heavily to the ground letting the serum slip from her hand.

Dracco's uncle who had followed us leapt in the air and neatly caught the vial in his hand.

Whew!

The vial was safe for the moment. But something else was

happening.

Madam Adela was twisting and turning in rage going 'HZZZZZZ' and then the scary and sinister shape of Buja the Sorceress emerged.

She hissed at Dracco's uncle like an angry snake and turned around to the petrified Dracco and screamed –

"YOU WILL BE MINE!"

"Not if I can help it," thundered Dracco's uncle.

He quickly opened the vial of serum and threw it at Buja the Sorceress.

Buja let out a terrible scream and the whole castle trembled.

She let out another howl as she tried to put her scrawny long fingers around the throat of Dracco's uncle.

Dracco's uncle quickly pushed her arm away and poured the rest of the serum over her.

There was a loud crash of thunder and lightning.

Then we saw her slowly disintegrate before our eyes.

One moment she was this wretched creature and the next moment her body had crumbled into a heap of black dust.

Dracco's uncle calmly clapped his hands and the black dust on the floor flew out of the window as if on wings.

The bats who had been peacefully sleeping rose up as a cacophonous black cloud and flew behind the black dust.

They rapidly pecked at the dust. Very soon there was not a speck of black dust visible in the sky.

Dracco's uncle hummed a tune and left the room wearing an evil smile.

What a cool customer he was! No way would I mess around with Dracco's uncle.

We kitties were joyful.

We patted Katski on the back and leapt about shouting -

Hip, Hip, Hurray!

04 Days Before Easter

Wednesday, Morning

We had had another exciting night!

As soon as I got back to our room, I had scribbled furiously all that I had seen.

On waking up, I read through my scribbled entries once again.

My poor diary! If this went on, I am sure it would be exhausted with all the excitement that I had been recording.

But I was determined to record every little detail.

I knew that the rest of the gang would arrive from London very soon.

What a lot we had to tell them!

I didn't want to miss one tiny detail.

Would they believe their ears when we told them everything that had happened and who we had met since coming to Bran Castle?

What about all our friends back home? My diary would be an exciting read for them as well.

Katski joined us for breakfast. We meowed it over with her.

Katski told us that the vial that Ivy had picked up was not the one containing the anti-vampire serum.

Dracco's uncle was aware of how Buja the Sorceress operated.

He knew well enough that she would be watching them and that as soon as he left the castle she would come rushing in – in another human form - to steal the vial.

He had been working since he returned to the castle and had developed a serum to turn sorcerers to dust.

He had pretended to leave the castle and had watched the whole scene as a Bat – hanging upside down in his bedroom.

Sure enough, Buja, now in the form of Ivy had come to befriend Dracco with the idea of stealing the anti-vampire serum.

The anti-serum serum had been hidden safely in another room. Dracco's uncle was waiting until midnight to use it as Dracco would then become 12 years old.

Once Buja in the form of Ivy was in his room, he had turned from a supposedly sleeping bat into Dracco's uncle once again.

He had then got a hold of Ivy, taken the vial from her hand and thrown the contents over her - destroying her forever.

Wow!

Who would believe this story?

I felt so amazed at these extraordinary revelations that I wondered if I had dreamt all of it.

But what mattered was that Dracco's uncle was able to save the anti-vampire serum and destroy the nasty sorceress who had been determined to turn Dracco into a vampire.

Her wish had been to increase the number of vampires in Transylvania so that she could rule over a larger kingdom of vampires.

Thankfully, she had not been a match for Dracco's uncle once he had got back his powers.

No wonder she had had him drugged and kidnapped by her Bujions and kept him locked up in her dungeon under a powerful bright light to weaken his powers.

The Bujions were terrified of Buja the Sorceress. They obeyed her commands only because she was evil and controlled them through fear and wicked deeds if they did not obey her.

03 Days Before Easter

Thursday, Morning

Just after breakfast, a huge limousine drove up.

Our friends had arrived!

Solo and Hobbs his manservant, with Monk and Terrance, leapt out of the car.

Very soon Polo jumped out followed by his family, Raoul and the Señora.

We rushed out to greet everyone! How glad we were to see

them.

What a lot we had to tell them.

Tomorrow the rest of the guests would be arriving and the Castle would be full.

Mom had planned a party for forty-five friends of her wealthy client.

Additional local staff had been hired and there was a lot of hustle and bustle going on in the Castle.

None of the humans had noticed the absence of Madam Adela.

The local assistants were so well trained that they just continued with their tasks as usual.

Of course, the side of castle that Katski occupied was out of bounds and not opened to the public.

We took our friends up to our room while the adults congregated in the dining room to discuss the party with Mom and Aunt Florence.

The party was scheduled for Easter Sunday but there would be fancy lunches and dinners starting from today.

Fromage was bursting to tell the tale of Katski and our adventures to Monk, Terrance and Polo.

He babbled on for a few minutes starting at the end, jumping to the middle and then rushing to the beginning.

I knew they couldn't make head nor tail of what Fromage was talking about in his excited state.

"Hold your horses, Fromage," I meowed.

"The best way to get the entire story so that Monk, Terrance and Polo can understand what happened - is to read the events I recorded in my diary."

So, I opened my diary and gave a reading of what had happened since our arrival at Bran Castle.

They heard our story in a bemused state.

I understood well their feelings of disbelief.

If I had not lived through it myself, I would have had difficulty believing this tale too.

02 Days Before Easter

Friday, Morning

We spent the morning showing Monk, Terrance and Polo the grave-yard at the back of the castle where Katski had played hide-and-seek with us.

The team spent a thoroughly lazy morning. As we didn't have a watch, we went in far too early for lunch, and were shooed out by Mom.

She scolded us saying "I don't know how you can come in at ten past twelve for a one o'clock lunch, honestly!"

We meowed as if she had not fed us for centuries, and she soon pulled out a lovely lunch.

Mom can never resist our pleading meows for very long.

She handed Terrance and Polo some fine bones and they were delighted.

We were happy campers!

We had had a good meal and we were with the people we loved best.

It had been agreed that the next day, being Easter Sunday, Mom would hide the Easter eggs very early in the morning before she started work on the party.

We were all looking forward to the Easter egg hunt.

Though, I must say that Terrance and Polo, being doggies, always seemed to have an edge over us kitties in locating the hidden Easter eggs.

From my point of view, to balance the contest, I said that they had to give us kitties a good 15 minutes advance start.

After much arguing, I had got them both to agree to my proposal.

One thing that I had noticed with dogs was that once I got my point of view across firmly
– they usually buckled down and accepted my wishes.

Dogs have an issue with authority whereas we cats are independent spirits.

I knew that THEY could never have convinced ME to give them a head start.

I kept the thought to myself.

No way did I wish to give them any ideas.

Katski had also invited us over for Dracco's big anti-vampire serum transformation.

I had managed to cajole Katski to agree to us bringing along

Monk, Terrance and Polo.

At first, she had agreed to Monk but had put her foot down when it came to Terrance and Polo.

With the greatest difficulty, with much cajoling and pleading, I had got her to agree to the doggies coming along as well.

After consultation with Dracco – who adored doggies, Katski had reluctantly agreed.

I somehow felt it was important for Monk, Terrance and Polo to meet Dracco and his uncle.

Polo is an excitable doggie who tended to believe anything I said.

But I had a feeling Monk and much-travelled Terrance, both who were well-read, found it hard to believe that vampires really existed.

That day pandemonium reigned in the castle with much activity.

All the guests had arrived. They roamed around the castle and grounds chatting amongst themselves.

Mom was run off her feet. But I knew that she would hide the

Easter eggs in the back grave- yard on Easter Sunday.

She was busy organizing the local staff to serve fresh delicious snacks throughout the morning, in addition to serving lunch and dinner.

All meals were to be five-course French meals and a seven-course meal was to be served at the final party dinner.

We kept out of everyone's way and spent the day lounging around in our room.

We didn't miss our meals though. How could we? Stomachs rule in the animal kingdom.

Happy tummies – happy kitties! That's our motto.

01 Day Before Easter

Saturday, Evening

The guests had gathered in the great hall and were being served champagne and wonderful French delicacies.

There was much laughter and merriment with music and dancing. Everyone seemed to be having a wonderful time.

The party had a costume theme and half the great hall was filled with Dracula-like imposters. Black seemed to be the chosen color for their clothing.

I smirked to myself. Ha! I thought. I knew the real Count Dracula and these imposters would not stand a chance next to him.

The food was being served by the spiffy waiters that Mom had hired, and we discretely snapped up all the delicious morsels that accidently dropped from the hands of the guests.

In keeping with the haunted theme, the lights were dimmed low, so Mom had no idea what we were up to.

Terrance, the well-behaved doggy detective, watched the party discretely from a corner.

He made no comment as the lot of us cautiously twirled in-and-out through the crowd, happily eating up all the glorious stuff that frequently fell to the ground.

Fromage was in his element!

Cara sat with Terrance as she had no interest in gobbling up leftovers, as she called the delicious delicacies that landed on the ground.

I joined Cara and Terrance after I had my fill.

I noticed that Terrance had his eyes glued on a tall lady dressed in a long black coat that reached her ankles, with her long blond hair piled on top of her head.

The tall lady was having a merry conversation with a large lady abundantly covered in jewelry.

What was Terrance up to? I thought to myself. Was he on duty?

I looked over at Solo to see what he was doing. He was conversing with a guest but his eyes kept flicking over the tall lady.

I smelled that something was up!

I decided to watch her myself. It was easy enough for me, as despite the darkness, I could see very well unlike either Solo or Terrance.

I leaned over to Terrance and said,

"Need some help, my friend?" Terrance startled, whispered back, "I have been told by Solo to keep an eye on that lady, but it's difficult to see much, as it's so dark in this great hall.

"Your assistance would be a great help"

I didn't need a second invitation. I softly moved over close to the two ladies and eavesdropped on their conversation.

The conversation revolved around the pudgy lady's wonder poodle, Fifi.

Apparently, Fifi was the smartest and most wonderful poodle in the world - very refined and elegant and had not joined the party as she needed her beauty sleep.

The tall lady was talking about Fifi who she had met earlier in the day and gushed over her beauty while the pudgy lady listened to her enthralled.

What a sucker, I thought to myself. Fifi sounded like a spoilt brat of a poodle.

Hey! Hey! Hey!

I couldn't believe my eyes.

The tall lady had bent over the pudgy lady, cooed in her ear and deftly removed a large shiny brooch from her dress without her noticing it.

I saw the tall lady neatly slip the brooch into her coat pocket as she continued to prattle on about the beauty of Fifi.

I dashed back to Terrance and gasped -

"That blond lady stole the brooch from that pudgy lady. I saw her hide the brooch in her pocket. I am sure of it."

As the tall, blond lady kissed the pudgy lady and left the great hall, Terrance sprang into action.

I followed Terrance to see what he would do.

Solo had watched Terrance leave and had followed us out to the long corridor leading to the foyer and the door.

Solo hailed the lady and before she could disappear out of the door pretending to be tipsy, handed her a glass of champagne, insisting that she enjoy the delicious golden liquid.

The lady curbed her impatience with a smile and accepted the glass.

I watched amazed at how nifty Terrance was.

In that short space of time, he had put his snout into the tall lady's long coat, had grabbed the brooch in his mouth and disappeared from the room.

The lady hardly noticed his sudden arrival and rapid disappearance.

What a marvelous detective team! I gloated to myself.

Bravo! Solo and Terrance.

Soon after, the lady excused herself and left the castle not aware that the brooch that she had deftly lifted off the pudgy lady's dress was no longer in her possession.

I went searching for Terrance, not only to congratulate him, but to also make him give me – my share of the kudos.

After all, it was I who had alerted him at the point when the lady had stolen the brooch.

I had thought that this was going to be a holiday for all of us. But I should have known better.

Solo and Terrance were always on duty. A party such as the one organized by Mom with plenty of rich people always drew jewel thieves and other crooks out of the woodwork.

For sure Solo would have been hired to keep an eye out for such thieves.

Sunday, Late evening

There had not been a ripple to disturb the party and everyone continued to enjoy themselves.

No one was aware that a major theft had been averted.

Solo had patted Terrance on the head, retrieved the valuable brooch and gone off to return it to the pudgy lady.

Terrance was off duty and could enjoy the rest of the evening.

Soon after that, the rest of the team joined us and we decided to take a walk by the flowing river at the bottom of the hill near the castle.

Since Terrance was with us and we were relatively close to the castle, I had no fears and did not miss Katski not being around.

It was good to get out into the fresh, cold air.

We strolled by the river as the water rushed onwards and downwards gently slurping and slapping into the banks of the river.

Our bedroom offered a three hundred and sixty degrees view as the castle sat on the very edge of an enormous cliff.

From our window, I had observed a sea of green tree tops and occasional silver threads where the river winded through the forest.

I had wished to explore the river the moment I had seen it from our window and here we were with our stomachs filled with Mom's glorious French cuisine.

There was a large full moon in the sky and the banks of the river were illuminated with the silvery beams of the moon.

The place was strangely quiet.

We decided to stop for a little while and enjoy the luminous moon.

We lay down on some rocks, very close to the water's edge and observed the big yellow moon and discussed if it was really made upof cheese.

Fromage was convinced that the moon was made up of fabulous cheese.

We listened with half-closed eyes to Fromage as he rambled on about the moon and speculating on what types of cheese, the moon was made of – and soon fell asleep.

We woke up to the rustling of some branches of the trees

around us.

Some creatures were moving about.

Terrance had sat up with his ears raised to attention.

He whispered, “Don’t make a sound!

“Hide under that big boulder, quick all of you – “Polo not a bark from you.”

We heard the urgency in his tone and I quickly pushed Cara, Charlotte and Fromage ahead of me and hid with Monk and Polo behind the great boulder.

We peered out from under the huge stone. The moon had hidden behind a cloud and it was very, very dark.

We couldn’t hear a thing other than the sudden howls of the wind and the hoot of an owl.

Why had Terrance asked us to hide?

Suddenly, the moon peeped out from behind a cloud and I saw what had alarmed Terrance.

It was a great big wolf. He was slurping the water from the river. He had not spotted us.

My blood rang cold and I whispered, "Don't move any one!

"Keep still!"

I saw that Terrance had moved away from us, to ensure that the wolf, if he did smell our presence, would only see him.

My esteem for Terrance, which was already high, reached epic proportions.

He was truly a very brave and wonderful friend.

But would he be able to fight a terrible wolf?

Terrance was a big and strong dog - skilled in the art of defense.

He was courageous with a brave heart.

But could he be compared to a wild wolf who provided himself with his daily food through his cunningness?

I could sense that everyone was terrified.

We crouched together hardly daring to breathe.

Never could one find such collective fear amongst a group of friends.

The moonlight gleamed on the wolf. The wolf had had his fill of water and sat on the bank observing the moon.

Suddenly, he let out a howl that made our blood curdle.

Where was his pack? I wondered. I knew that wolves moved around in packs.

Was this a lone ranger?

As if in response to my thoughts, there were several howls from somewhere deep in the forest. He was not alone.

Horror of horrors! Was he calling the rest of the pack to come join him? Terrance would never be able to withstand a pack of wolves.

I was paralyzed with fear for both Terrance and ourselves.

Then abruptly, the wolf stopped howling.

He had caught sight of a large black cloud descending on him. A whole colony of bats swarmed and circled above his head.

The air was thick with bats of all sizes.

The wolf was blinded by the flapping wings of this huge

colony of bats.

He did not wait to study his surroundings, but raced off to join the rest of his pack.

He flew like a bullet out of sight.

We watched in wonder as the colony of bats circled around for a few minutes more and then swiftly flew away.

The sky was still again.

We collapsed in a heap as Terrance came to us and started licking us in relief.

I cannot stand licks from doggies, but I let him lick us knowing that this was a way for him to express his relief.

He took his responsibilities as protector of his pals very seriously.

We quickly scampered back to the castle, all together, in case the whole wolf pack decided to come for a drink of water from the river.

What a stroke of luck that the colony of bats had descended just at the correct time.

They had saved us.

Sunday, Night

We were heartened to hear the merrymakers at the party. It was a relief to note some normalcy after our terrifying ordeal.

But we didn't want to hang around for long.

Avoiding the crowd, we silently trotted over to Katski's side of the castle.

We wished to show our friends who had just arrived, all the interesting nooks and crannies that we had come to know through Katski.

It was quiet when we arrived at Katski's quarters.

There was a hush about the place unlike at the party we had just left where the guests were noisily enjoying themselves.

Dracco looked nervous and even Dracco's uncle appeared paler than usual - which was deathly white.

Katski whispered that Dracco's uncle was worried that the

anti-vampire serum wouldn't work. But Katski was confident it would.

So far, he had never known Dracco's uncle to prepare any concoction that had not worked. Still there was tension until the whole ceremony was completed.

Dracco caught Polo's eye and he cheered up instantly.

Polo is a young Pekinese pup, good-natured and kind.

His little pink tongue hung out and he loved playing with kids.

Katski jealously watched Polo as he ran around Dracco while his little nails click-clacked on the teak floors.

She had a superior air about her and I knew what she was thinking –

"What a silly little half-pint."

However, Dracco' s pensive expression had turned to delight and he started throwing a ball to Polo to fetch.

Polo fetched the ball, and dropped it at Dracco' s feet and looked at him as if to say, "do it again pal".

"Look on the bright side Katski," I meowed.

"At least Polo has taken his mind off Ivy and her treachery as well as tonight's ordeal."

"You are right, oh wise-one!" responded Katski to me with a smile and she forgot her jealousy.

There was no doubt about it – Katski loved Dracco and of

course Dracco loved Katski.

Saturday, Mid-Night

Dracco's uncle suddenly appeared and said – "The time has come Dracco.

"COME!"

Dracco's eyes were as big as saucers.

I knew that the moment had arrived for the transformation.

Dracco slowly put down the ball he was about to throw for Polo to fetch and scooped up Katski into his arms.

He slowly followed his uncle out of the room.

We trailed behind him to see what an anti- vampire transformation ceremony was all about.

We entered another large room.

The room was dimly lit with candles sparsely placed around the room.

There were bats all over the place -some hanging upside down.

Others were silently floating in the air, their black silhouettes casting spooky shadows in the candlelight.

I heard a low squeak of fear coming out of Polo and Terrance shushed him and pulled him closer to him.

Monk, unknown to himself, also drew closer to Terrance.

The rest of us of course had already gone through a similar ordeal when we went to rescue Dracco's uncle from the dungeon of the now terminated Buja, the Sorceress.

But I could understand the creepy feeling of our friends who had not gone through this nerve-wracking experience before.

There was a solitary small coffin open in the middle of the room.

Dracco's uncle led Dracco to it and lifted him into the coffin.

Dracco closed his eyes and crossed his arms across his chest.

From nowhere came a low deep hum.

I looked around to see where the sound was coming from.

I noticed that the flying bats had all descended and were hanging from the rafters of the ceiling.

They were making a strange sing-song hum.

It's as if they knew something was about to happen and were humming as one choir.

This strange hum put Dracco into a deep sleep.

Katski who was cuddled up against Dracco was gently lifted out of the coffin and placed on the floor by Dracco's uncle.

Dracco's uncle then raised his arms and there was total silence.

The humming stopped.

We ourselves were rooted to the ground.

We watched silently with saucer-like eyes. There was not a peep from anyone of us.

Katski who had been reluctant to leave Dracco's side watched Dracco's uncle like a statue with shining eyes.

It was only I, keen to record the goings-on in my diary, who dared to take in everything and carefully memorized what went on.

Dracco's uncle raised the vial containing the anti-vampire serum and scattered it over the now, deep asleep, Dracco.

There was a flash of lightening and a deep roar of thunder.

We all automatically moved back and brave Terrance crouched in front of all of us while we cowered under a large table right against the wall.

We peered fearfully from behind Terrance – mesmerized with what was happening before us.

The small coffin containing Dracco's body had a flame surrounding it.

Dracco's uncle roared –

"DRACULA COMMANDS YOU

– LEAVE – LEAVE – LEAVE!"

Dracco's uncle was Dracula!!!

This is what I had suspected all along!

There was another crash of thunder and we saw a dark stream of dust leave Dracco's body and float towards the window!

The army of bats came to life and with one swoop went after the dust pecking at it furiously until every speck disappeared.

SILENCE!

We dared not move.

We hid huddled together under the table, hearts pounding.

I heard Monk whisper – "That's Count Dracula?"

Polo whimpered and covered his nose with his paws.

Even Terrance seemed rattled.

Katski seemed to get a new lease of life and she dashed over to the small coffin and leaped onto Dracco.

She desperately started licking his face meowing pathetically.

We watched helplessly.

Even the usual voluble Fromage seemed struck dumb.

Dracula crouched on his knees exhausted, his arm around Dracco while Katski desperately tried to wake up Dracco.

Suddenly Dracco stirred.

Katski stopped her licking and crouched silently on Dracco's chest while Count Dracula slowly rose to his feet.

Count Dracula gently lifted Dracco's lips and studied his teeth.

Terrance whispered –

"He is examining Dracco's teeth to see if his canine teeth are still long and pointed –

"The first signs of a vampire." We held our breath!

Dracula sighed with relief and patted Katski on the head and said –

"Dracco is fine, Katski – you can relax.

"He will be up and playing with you in the garden tomorrow."

With a salute to us – and in a flash, Dracula turned into a large BAT.

With a WHOOOSH – he flapped his wings and flew out of the window into the night followed by his large army of bats.

It was only at that moment that I realized that it was Dracula in the form of a bat and his colony of bat fiends who had saved us from the wolf.

The last to leave was a little baby bat.

Was I dreaming or was he a little vampire bat? He seemed to be smiling at me!

No, it couldn't be possible. I must have imagined it!

Did he grin at me before flying off?

I observed my friends:

- Terrance stood up with an anxious look on his face.
- Monk had a bemused expression as well.
- Polo could not contain himself any longer and went –

"Woof, woof, woof, woof!"

I felt a certain sense of satisfaction.

Now, they had to believe what I had recorded in my diary!

They had witnessed a real live Vampire in action.

They would have to salute my – VAMPIRE DIARY!

No question about that!

As for me, I was of the same opinion as Katski
– I admired Count Dracula.

I was ever so grateful that he had saved us from the wolf.

Easter Sunday

Morning:

I was glad that we had helped Count Dracula escape to help Dracco.

I looked around at my family and friends gathered around the long dining table in the kitchen.

I felt so lucky to have good friends and a loving family.

We had learned from Katski that Dracco's uncle was a real Count.

Our humans were having breakfast and we were having ours too when Katski andDracco joined us.

Dracco could now go out during the daytime and he was delirious with joy.

Friendship counts in big ways and small ways, I decided.

Without good friends, life would not only be boring but also lonely.

I thought back to our life together –

- The first time we met Monk and Terrance.
- How we befriended Polo.
- The mysteries that we had solved together.

This time around, there was no large mystery to be solved except the small incident with the jewelry theft. But we had helped a tormented little boy and his beloved cat to become happy and in the process had an exceptional and great adventure.

Looking at my friends, I counted on my paws the value of friendship.

I could come up with quite a few:

No matter how much trouble one of us got into – the others would always be there to save him or her.

Monk always shared his full cream milk with all of us.

Terrance allowed me to head Inca & Company, our detective agency, even though he was a detective doggy long before I even thought of becoming a detective.

Fromage laughed at every ones' jokes – however terrible they were.

When it was cold, there was always someone ready to cuddle up to you to keep the cold away.

When one of us was frightened, she or he had company to cope with the fright.

After breakfast we all ran into the backyard. Mom had already

hidden the Easter eggs.

She shouted "Ready, steady, go!" – to start off the Easter egg hunt.

We kitties raced off to search for the eggs while Terrance and Polo patiently waited for the 15 minutes advance period to be over.

Mom gave a puzzled look as to why they were not joining the search – but rushed off as she had a busy day ahead of her.

Despite our lead, the doggies found most of the Easter eggs first.

But no worries!

They shared the chocolate Easter eggs with us – that's how they are – these doggy friends of ours.

Generous and loyal to a fault!

We had a fun morning amongst the tombstones in the grave-yard.

We were going to miss this gloomy butexciting place.

Bran Castle had grown upon us.

After lunch, we went over to Katski and Dracco's place.

Dracco's uncle – Count Dracula was fast asleep in his coffin.

His bat buddies were fast asleep as well.

He did look peaceful, sleeping in his coffin, his long fangs visible even in his sleep.

We left him to sleep and continued on to Dracco and Katski's room.

Katski told us that Dracco would be attending the village school as soon as the holidays were over.

He hoped that Dracco would meet friends of his own age.

I remembered Dracco's last friend Ivy. She had been sweet until we found out that she was actually Buja the Sorceress.

Katski was confident that Dracco would find some nice friends when he started school.

We lounged around while Polo played catch with Dracco.

Not only were we going to miss the Castle but we were going to miss our new friends – Katski, Dracco and his fabulous uncle – Count Dracula.

Count Dracula would always be my hero!

That night while Mom and our human friends were at the party which was in full swing, Count Dracula woke up and took us on a trek into the jungle.

It was shadowy outside with thick clouds that were hiding all the pretty stars.

It was silent and still – not a sound to be heard other than the howling wind in the trees and the distant water gloomily flowing in the river down below.

There was not even a peep from a hooting owl or the sound of a hedgehog scampering in the drains.

The last time we trekked out of Bran Castle we had been shivering with fright.

But tonight, in the company of Count Dracula, his army of bats and Terrance, we felt safe and secure.

Our wanderings soon stopped as we arrived at the familiar Tomb.

There were a bunch of Bujions outside.

I looked about anxiously wondering if we should hide and why Count Dracula had brought us here after our last experience with this place.

But I needn't have worried.

They were all lounging about in a happy and relaxed state.

As soon as they saw the Count – their grins broadened as they babbled –

"Welcome, Count Dracula.

"All the arrangements have been made to thank you and your friends for saving us from the cruel and evil sorceress – Buja."

We followed them into the tomb curious to see what was going on.

The previously musty and dirty corridor was spotless.

The Bujions excitedly led us into their hall which was now gleaming and full of food platters on a long large table in the center.

There was a group of Bujions with various musical instruments ready to be played.

As soon as we arrived, the conductor of the group gave a signal and there was happy music that invaded the hall.

All the Bujions started dancing and the music was so tempting that I couldn't help but say to my friends –

"Let's join them."

No one needed a second invitation.

Without further ado we all started dancing while the band played wonderful music.

Even Count Dracula couldn't help but sway to the lively music.

No doubt about it – I thought to myself – no better way to end a story other than with a dance!

OLE! OLE!! OLE!!!

A Very Happy Easter

To All The Readers Of My Diary

R.F. Kristi invites you to free books, news and much more.

Please sign up via:

www.incabookseries.com

If you enjoyed this book, please leave a review on Amazon or Goodreads. Positive reviews help a great deal.

Thank you.

Inca Book Series:

- **The Cats Who Crossed Over from Paris**
- **Christmas Cats**
- **Cats in Provence**
- **Ninja Spy Cats**
- **Diary of a Snoopy Cat**

R.F. KRISTI'S INCA BOOK SERIES
Award-Winner in the Wishing Shelf Book Awards & Reader's Favorite Awards

"**The Verdict:** It's pretty easy to recommend the Inca Book Series. The books are fun, interesting, and well-illustrated and provide a great deal of value. The characters are fantastic and the stories are even better. The French cultural influence is a real positive for me as well because that's such a rarity and I think it's great for kids to learn about other countries and cultures. **The Illustrations:**
... The illustrations rank right up there....... The characters are all incredibly cute .... The style of these illustrations is unique. I can't think of another book we've reviewed here at Kids Fun Channel that looks anything like this. I simply love the cats, their expressions, and how much these illustrations add to the fun found in this book."

Kids Fun Channel

Connect online

www.incabookseries.com

rfkristibooks@gmail.com

The author supports the Cat Protection Trust of Sri Lanka

https://www.facebook.com/CatProtection-Trust/

PLEASE JOIN IN SUPPORTING THE CAT PROTECTION TRUST OF SRI LANKA

CPSIA information can be obtained
at www.ICGtesting.com
Printed in the USA
FSHW04n0712130418
46929FS

9 780998 429113